For Jamie and Arley – PJ

First published in 2013

Allen & Unwin
83 Alexander Street, Crows Nest NSW 2065, Australia
Phone: (61 2) 8425 0100,
Email: info@allenandunwin.com
Web: www.allenandunwin.com

A Cataloguing-in-Publication entry is available from the
National Library of Australia: www.trove.nla.gov.au

ISBN 978 1 74331 140 0

Design by Andrew Weldon and Bruno Herfst
Set in 12 pt Dolly

This book was printed in June 2013 at McPherson's Printing Group,
76 Nelson St, Maryborough, Victoria 3465, Australia.
www.mcphersonsprinting.com.au

10 9 8 7 6 5 4 3 2 1

Paul Jennings & *Andrew Weldon*

DON'T LOOK NOW

BOOK TWO

ALLEN&UNWIN
SYDNEY · MELBOURNE · AUCKLAND · LONDON

Story One

A MAGICIAN NEVER TELLS

1

Grounded

'**You're grounded, Ricky,**' **said Mum.**

'Yes,' said Dad. 'In more ways than one.' He gave me a meaningful look.

'No movies.'

'What?'

'No Macca's.'

'That's cruel.'

'No swimming.'

'Give me a break.'

Mum grabbed my phone and put it in her pocket.

'No phone.'

I let my face do the talking.

Mum snorted and walked out of the room.

Dad waited until she was out of earshot.
'And no, you know what,' he whispered.

'Oh, Dad…'

He cut me off. 'I mean it, Ricky. No flying.'

I stomped up to my bedroom and went over the whole thing in my mind. It was so unfair.

There was something wrong with me. I didn't belong to the tribe. I was an outsider. I always wandered around at lunch time on my own. It was almost as if I were invisible.

I was lonely. I didn't have one special friend.
And I wanted one. A very special person.

And that very special person was…

It was because of her that I was grounded.

Dad was driving into the automatic car wash when I spotted her. She was so cool sitting there with dark sunglasses and a high ponytail, listening to music.

I really wanted to say hello. Badly. So badly that
I forgot where we were.

I got soaked. Dad got soaked. And the seats of the car were ruined. And Dad bumped his head. And the car stopped, and wouldn't start again.

So I was grounded.

And worst of all – the car-wash girl must have seen everything.

I mooched around home for a while and tried to think of a way out of my problem. Maybe if I sucked up to Dad he would cancel my punishment for the car-wash incident.

He was a pretty soft-hearted bloke really. And the only other person in the world who could fly.

Dad wasn't perfect. But I loved him.

'I'm sorry, Ricky,' said Dad. 'But your mother is upset about the car seats getting ruined. You have to stay home. You are grounded. You can't leave the house.'

SOME THINGS YOU SHOULD KNOW ABOUT **MUM**.

• Big brain. _____

• Gives impression she knows what you've been up to, even if you haven't been up to anything. ___

• Nice nose. Could have been a nose model. ___

• Supersonic Mum hearing. Can hear naughtiness five rooms away. ___

• Has embarrassing nicknames for me. Worst: `Baby boy'. ___

And we both knew you couldn't argue with Mum when she was angry.

I looked down at my shoes and sniffed.
Dad put his hand on my shoulder.

'Why don't you put your tent up in the backyard?' he said. 'That might be fun.'

2

Going Up

It was a warm night and I could see the stars through the flap of my tent. Mum's black-petal poppies were invisible, but I knew they were growing down near the back fence.

It was good in the tent, but not much fun on my own.

I concentrated hard.

'Up,' I said.

I lifted myself about thirty centimetres and plopped down.

'Up,' I said again.

Nothing happened. It was hard work flying. I always got tired after a while. I couldn't just stay in the air forever.

I wished that someone could see me.

Someone did.

'Ouch,' I yelled.

'Sorry,' said Dad. 'I didn't know you would be flying. You have to be careful, Ricky. No one must see you fly. I've told you a thousand times. If you are seen you will fall to the ground.'

'There's no one around,' I said.

'What about Mum?' he said. 'She might see you.'

I nodded. 'Why can't we tell her that we can fly?'
I asked.

'Think about it,' said Dad. 'If she saw me flying
way up high and I fell to my death because of her –
how would she feel?'

'Guilty,' I said. 'She would feel guilty.'

'Right,' said Dad. 'She would never get over it. So these days I don't fly if I don't have to. It's better that she doesn't know.'

I felt sad. I didn't like Mum being left out of it. After all, we were a family.

'I want to tell her,' I said.

Dad shook his head and changed the subject.

'You are meant to be totally grounded, but you
also need to practise flying. Promise me you won't
fly more than a few centimetres off the ground.
It's too dangerous.'

'But, Dad. There must be a way to show people I can fly. There has to be. I really want to be…

Dad sighed. 'Sleep well, Ricky,' he said.

He crawled out of the tent and vanished into the night.

I zipped the tent closed to keep out any visitors. Creepy, crawly visitors.

I was scared of snakes.

We lived in a country town. Even though there were houses all around us, snakes sometimes came into our backyard.

What if I woke up in the night and found I had company?

Maybe a red-bellied black or a tiger snake.

I shuddered.

Fortunately it was a good tent with a sewn-in floor and an aluminium frame. I was safe and snug inside.

I clicked off my torch. I thought about the school concert that was coming up. What if I could fly in front of the whole school? I fell asleep, dreaming of fame and glory.

3

Booked Out

The next day I put my books into my backpack and walked to school thinking about the concert. It was being held to raise money for flood victims. If I could go on the stage and fly in front of everyone they would probably faint with shock. I would definitely be famous.

But I couldn't fly if someone was looking. I wouldn't even be able to get off the ground.

And I couldn't get *far* off the ground if I was carrying something. Even wet clothes had made it hard to fly. And the little dog I had saved seemed to weigh a tonne.

I made my way into a clearing in the trees. I looked around for inquisitive eyes. No dogs. No cats. No people.

What about birds? I couldn't see any, but Dad said you could never be sure that a whole flock of them wouldn't suddenly arrive.

I decided to give it a try. I looked up at a branch of a tree high above.

'Fly,' I said to myself.

I lifted a few centimetres off the ground.

'Higher,' I said.

Nothing happened. I hovered just off the ground, but I couldn't get higher.

I went up a little bit more – just a smidgen.

What was wrong? Why couldn't I get up to that branch? I had flown higher than that before when I chased the owl. In the night. In the nude.

My brain was boiling. My skull felt like the shell of a hand grenade about to go off. But nothing happened. I gave it one last desperate try.

It was no use. Why couldn't I do it?
What was different?

Of course.

The books. They were weighing me down.

'Down,' I said to myself.

I plopped onto the grass and shrugged off my backpack.

'Up,' I commanded. Slowly, slowly, I lifted up. Up and up and up. It was a long way down to the ground and I could hear a bird chirping in the bushes. If I fell I would be history. The branch was just above my head, but I decided it was too risky to be so far off the ground in a public place.

'Down,' I said reluctantly. I landed gently on the grass.

I needed to practise. Like Dad said. It's just like running or weight-lifting or anything. You get better if you practise.

I looked at the books in my bag. There was a big one about birds. Heavy.

'Up,' I said. I rose about half a metre.

'Higher.'

I lifted a little more. I could feel the blood boiling in my brain. It was too much for me.

'Down,' I said. I plopped down on to the grass, exhausted.

I took out the books and examined them.

'Every day,' I said to myself. 'I am going to fly with a bit more weight. I have to practise. Build up my brain power. Overcome the brain strain.'

4

Magic

When I reached school I called in at the office and asked for the form for the school concert.

I didn't know what to put.

I couldn't write *singing* because I couldn't sing. I couldn't write *acting* because I couldn't act. I couldn't write *weight-lifting* because I was as weak as a kitten.

And I couldn't write *flying* because I couldn't fly ·
in front of a dog let alone the whole school.

I licked the end of my pencil and wrote one word.

SCHOOL CONCERT
NAME
ACT
Toby Tilsit
Cheese Ventriliquism
Serena Plunket
Teacher Imitations
LESLEY STRANGE
SPEED EATING
Max Renquist
Trained Parrot
Isabella L'Amour
SCAT SINGING
'CHOIR ON FIRE'!!!
Brendan B.
JUGGLING
JAMES MALONEY
Sax
Ricky Sparrow
MAGIC

When I got home Mum and Dad already knew
that I had signed up for an act. One of the canteen
mothers had told Mum.

'I didn't know you could do magic,' said Mum.

'Neither did I,' said Dad in a suspicious voice.

'Pick a card. Any card,' I said.

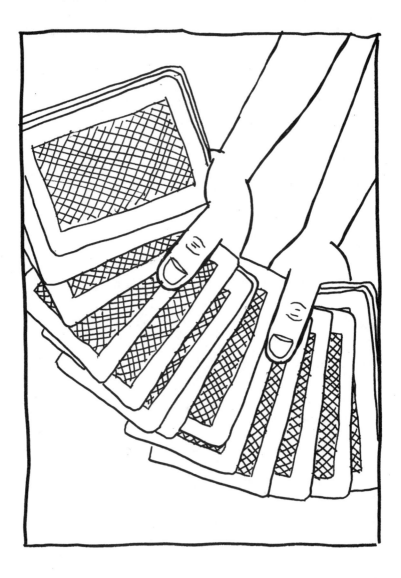

'King of spades,' I said.

'It is too,' she said. 'How did you know which card I picked?'

Dad grinned and took it out of her hand and ran his finger over the king of spades.

'Yes,' he said. 'How did you do that?'

'A magician never tells,' I said with a wink.

I walked to my room and threw the pack on the table.

Dad stuck his head around the door.

'Do you think it's a good enough trick to do in front of five hundred kids?' he said.

'Probably not,' I said. 'They'll boo me off the stage, won't they?'

He nodded sadly.

After he left I took my backpack and went down to my little tent with a pile of books and comics. I crawled inside and zipped up the fly.

The tent was a good place to practise flying because no one could see me. I couldn't go very high in there, but I could work on lifting heavy weights. It was good exercise for my brain.

The top comic was one of my favourite stories.

I still had to build up my stamina.
I had to be able to fly like a hero.

'Up,' I said to myself.

I rose about thirty centimetres. But it was an effort. I only lasted for about one minute then I had to come down for a rest. I waited for a while and tried again with the comics and two books. Up I went. I timed myself with my watch. Four minutes. Great – an improvement already.

I wrote my achievements in a little exercise book. I would try again the following day.

So that's how it went for the next two weeks. Every day after school I crept down to the tent with my books and comics and other heavy items I found around the house.

Each time I carefully checked the inside to make sure no creatures were watching. Then I zipped the tent closed and levitated carrying weights. I was safe. No prying eyes could see me.

HEAVINESS TRAINING (© RICKY)

DAY 1 ┤ Pile of comics
DAY 2 ┤ Dad's hammer
DAY 3 ┤ Cricket gear
DAY 4 ┤ Brick
DAY 5 ┤ Watermelon
DAY 6 ┤ Bowling ball
DAY 7 ┤ Big bottle of oil from kitchen.
DAY 8 ┤ 4ℓ tin of pineapple juice.
DAY 9 ┤ Electric jaffle maker, kettle
DAY 10 ┤ Old car battery
DAY 11 ┤ Bag of rocks.
DAY 12 ┤ Bag of rocks + dirt clumps.
DAY 13 ┤ Dictionary + big cookbook
DAY 14 ┤ Dictionary + big cookbook + bucket of water.

After two weeks I could lift really heavy stuff and hover for five minutes. Sometimes my brain would start to boil and I would have to come down for a rest. But eventually I was ready to fly to the top of a tree with a full backpack. The only trouble would be making sure that no animal or person saw me.

Finally the day of the big concert arrived. It was time to do my magic act on stage in front of the whole school.

'Do you think you're ready?' said Mum.

She didn't think my card trick was good enough, but she was too polite to say anything.

'Show us again,' she said.

I took out the pack of cards. 'Pick a card,' I said. 'Any card.'

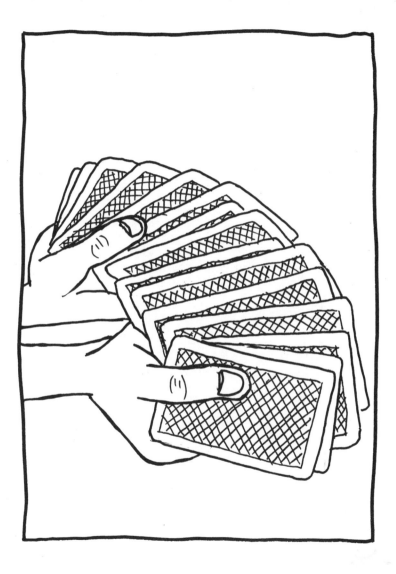

Mum took a card. She showed it to Dad, but not to me.

'It's the king of spades,' I said.

'How did you do it?' asked Mum.

'A magician never tells,' I said.

Dad took the pack from my hand and shuffled through them.

'It's an old trick,' he said. 'It's a one-act wonder.'

He was right. No one would fall for it.

I took the cards and put them in my backpack.

I didn't take any books to school. I had a different load to carry. Dad was waiting at the gate.

'I know you're up to something,' he said.

'A magician never tells,' I said.

He just nodded and gave me a knowing look.

'Remember your promise,' he said. 'No high flying.'

I nodded.

5

Stage Fright

It was a long way to school, but I finally got there. The day dragged on and on until it was time for the concert.

The hall was jammed with kids. It was packed. The usual mob of stirrers sat up the back ready to give a hard time to any weak acts.

I had stage fright. I wanted to turn around and run home.

The first act was the school choir. They sang four songs and after every one they got good applause – especially after the last one which was a heavy metal number. Next was a kid who had a solo act. He was a school prefect and it wasn't a bad effort. He got great applause.

After the juggling act it was James Maloney, the school captain. He was a really good-looking kid and very popular.

Everyone clapped like crazy when he had finished playing the saxophone – especially the girls. So far no one had been booed.

Finally it was my turn. Mr Wethers, the school principal, read out my name. I walked up to the microphone.

'I'm doing a magic trick,' I said.

I walked off the side of the stage and grabbed my little tent which I had stashed there. It was already erected. I dragged it into the middle of the stage and climbed inside. I zipped myself in and sat down in my usual spot.

Now I couldn't see anyone. But I could hear them.

'Quiet,' I heard Mr Wethers say. 'Give him a go.'

No one took any notice. The babbling from the audience continued. No one could see me. All they could see was a small tent on the stage.

'Up,' I said to myself.

Slowly I rose a little. I could feel my brain starting to bubble with the effort. But it was okay. The practice was paying off.

'Forward,' I said. I moved forward a little.

The noise outside grew less.

Then it stopped altogether.

'Higher,' I said.

'Forward.'

'Faster.'

'Circle.'

'Faster.'

It was time to end the act.

'Back,' I said to myself.

'Down.'

I landed with a gentle thud and climbed out of the tent. I bowed to the audience.

I was a hero again. The applause went on and on and on. Finally I left the stage and sat in the front row. People reached over and patted me on the back.

There were another seven acts and most of them were pretty good.

Finally Mr Wethers called me up to the stage.

'There can only be one winner,' he said. 'All the acts were good, but I think we can safely say that Ricky deserves the prize.'

He handed me a cheque for one hundred dollars. But I gave it back to him.

'For the flood victims,' I said.

There was more applause. Then Mr Wethers called for silence.

'I have some ideas, but I don't know how you did it, Ricky,' he said. 'It was a fantastic act. A little dangerous perhaps. I don't think any of us have seen a flying tent before. Lucky it didn't fall on someone's head. I don't suppose you are going to let us in on your secret.'

I shook my head.

'A magician never tells,' I said.

6

Who Me?

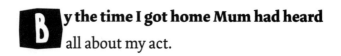**y the time I got home Mum had heard** all about my act.

'How did you do it?' she said. 'What was the trick?'

I took out my pack of cards.

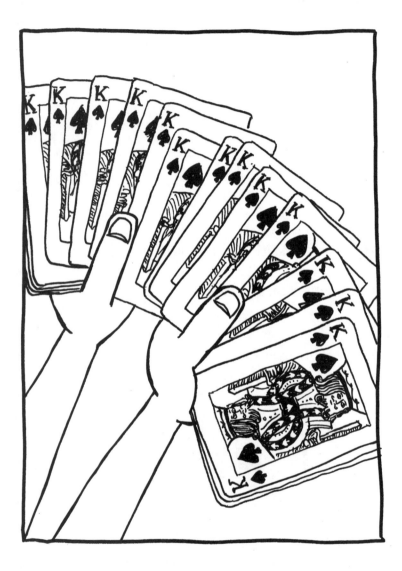

'All the cards were the same,' I said.

'Not that,' she yelled. 'You know what I mean. How did you make that tent fly?'

I didn't answer. Instead I ran up the stairs, pretending not to hear.

I heard the sound of music. Mum had turned on the TV. She never missed an episode of *Doctor Who*.

It would be safe to do a little flying. I threw open my window. 'Ricky coming up,' I yelled.

'Ricky coming up,' came back Dad's voice.

I flew up to the roof to get my lecture from Dad.

It was going to be a big one.

But it was worth it.

Story Two

ELEPHANT BONES

1

Buried Treasure

'There's an elephant in our backyard,' said Dad.

'What?' I yelled. I rushed over to the kitchen window and looked out.

'Rubbish,' said Mum.

'There's nothing there,' I said.

'Not a live elephant,' said Dad. 'A dead one.'

'Where? I can't see anything.'

'It's buried,' he said.

I sat down and Mum and I both went back to munching our muesli. We stared at him with raised eyebrows.

'No, really,' said Dad. 'I met an old guy who used to own this land. A farmer. He owned all the farms around here before there were any houses.'

'You don't get a lot of elephants around this neck of the woods,' said Mum scornfully. 'And elephants were never used on farms.'

'It was in the old days,' said Dad. 'A circus came to town. The elephant was doing tricks and it…'

His voice trailed away as we each imagined how the poor thing met its end.

'It's buried around here somewhere,' said Dad.

'Fantastic,' I shouted. 'I'm going to find it.'

'No you're not,' said Mum. 'No one's digging in my backyard.' She was using that sort of voice that tells you a storm is coming.

'I think you mean, *our* backyard,' said Dad.

'I've just planted five more black-petal poppies,' said Mum in a loud voice. 'And weeded the garden beds. And mowed the lawn. You two haven't done a...'

'Okay, okay,' said Dad. 'We get the picture.'

Mum was planning to grow around a hundred black-petal poppies. She was hoping to make a lot of money out of them.

But it would take time. So far she had earned enough for a new microwave.

The elephant skeleton could be worth something. That's what I was thinking. So was Dad.

Mum wasn't too keen about my idea. 'Elephants are protected,' she said.

'But this one has been dead for forty years,' said Dad. 'And it died of old age.'

He gave Mum a little kiss on the cheek.

'If we found the elephant skeleton we could sell it,' he said. 'We could use the money to buy a bigger TV. And pay for Ricky's swimming lessons.'

'We could bolt the bones together,' I yelled.

'And put it in the front yard,' said Dad excitedly.

ELEPHAS MAXIMUS

Mum snorted. 'You two are hopeless. I can never work out which of you is the biggest kid. There's not going to be any digging in my backyard.'

After breakfast I walked around the lawn looking for signs of an elephant grave. There were a few places where the ground had sunken a bit, but I couldn't dig there. Mum would be on to it straight away.

I looked behind the tool shed.

The weeds were long and tangled and there was a rusty bike and a broken washing machine. A high brick wall ran along the boundary. Dad built it so no one could see in.

'I didn't want anyone to see me practising flying,' Dad had told me. 'I used to sneak into the backyard when your mother was asleep and have a little fly around.'

My mind started to wander. I wanted to be…

I wanted to be in all the papers. On TV. I wanted to be googled.

If people knew what I could do everyone in the world would know my name. But no one was allowed to know that I could fly.

The dead elephant was the next best thing. If I found the skeleton I would be famous for that. Especially if we put it in the front yard for all to see. Fantastic.

The skeleton might be buried behind the shed. I could dig there and Mum would never know.

I fetched some tools.

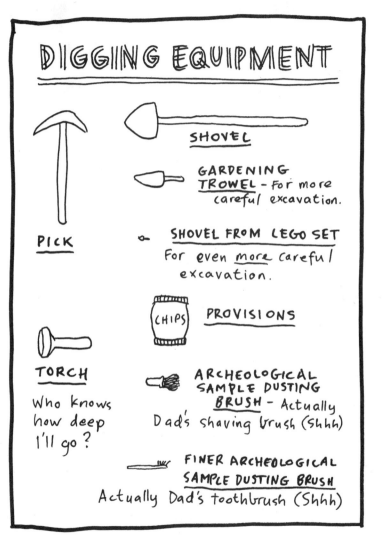

DIGGING EQUIPMENT

SHOVEL

GARDENING TROWEL - For more careful excavation.

PICK

SHOVEL FROM LEGO SET
For even more careful excavation.

PROVISIONS

CHIPS

TORCH

Who knows how deep I'll go?

ARCHEOLOGICAL SAMPLE DUSTING BRUSH - Actually Dad's shaving brush (Shhh)

FINER ARCHEOLOGICAL SAMPLE DUSTING BRUSH
Actually Dad's toothbrush (Shhh)

I started to dig. It was difficult work. The ground was hard and full of stones. After half an hour I was only a few centimetres down. I stopped for a rest. That's when I heard it.

Singing.

2

Siren Song

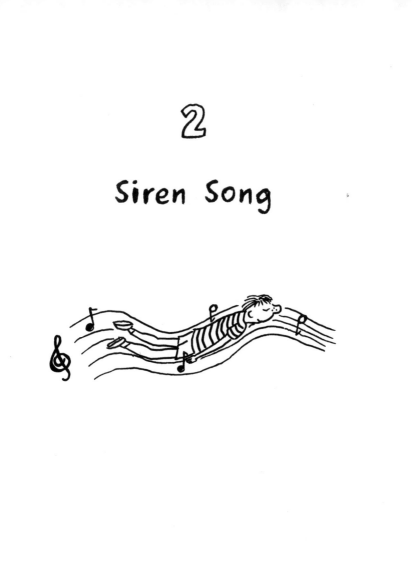

A girl's voice filled the air like a sweet scent. Images of chocolate, lemonade and jellybeans floated through my head. It was the voice of an angel. Oh, where was she? Who was she?

The singer of this wondrous song.

A strange feeling came over me.

The singing was coming from the other side of the garden wall.

I looked up. The wall was about four metres high. New people had moved in there, but I hadn't met them yet.

The beautiful sound continued. I wanted to see the face of this angel. I wanted to know her name. I wanted to hear her say my name.

I wished that I could peer over the wall. But we had no ladder.

'Don't need one,' Dad once said to me.

Mum had given him a funny look. He winked at me when she wasn't looking.

I put down my spade. I could take the risk of flying up to the top of the wall, but what if the beautiful singer saw me? Or what if Mum did? I would drop like a stone, the secret would be out and I would end up with a broken leg, or worse.

In the end I decided to risk it. Mum couldn't see me because the shed was blocking her view from the kitchen window.

I took a deep breath and concentrated.

Oh, what. I couldn't believe it. Wow. I rubbed my eyes.

It was her.

SOME THINGS YOU SHOULD KNOW ABOUT **CAR-WASH GIRL**.

• Probably a really nice person I reckon.

• Hair the colour of Macca's chips.

• Ace forehead.

• Pointy nose. Not in a bad way.

• Vaguely friendly, despite never having smiled at me.

• Shoes — probably the right brand.

I lowered myself so that only my head showed above the wall. I hung on with my fingers so that if I dropped I wouldn't fall down and break a leg.

Or worse.

'Hi, there,' I said to the car-wash girl.

She didn't answer. Maybe she couldn't hear me. Or she was ignoring me. I opened my mouth to shout. But the words froze in my mouth. And my heart almost stopped when I saw what was on the other side of her yard.

A digging machine stood silent guard beside the hole.

I gasped and ducked out of sight. I floated down and landed gently next to my own hole.

There was no doubt about it. My neighbours were looking for the elephant too. And the girl with the expensive sunglasses and the beautiful voice was in on it.

The cheek of it. I was really annoyed with her. The first time I'd tried to talk to her, I'd ended up grounded for ruining the car. And now she was after my elephant bones.

The elephant could easily be buried in their backyard. And they had a digging machine.

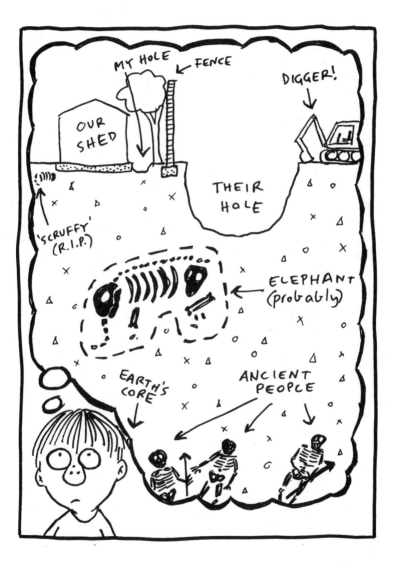

I picked up the spade and made a few dejected stabs at my hole. But it was no good. The ground was too hard. I felt so miserable.

I wanted to find the elephant skeleton for Mum. But the new neighbours had a digger. How could I compete with that?

As if to answer my question a growling engine cleared its throat and sprang into life. Blue smoke from its exhaust floated over the wall. I was filled with anger and disappointment. Without thinking I flew straight up.

I had been seen.

Instantly I felt myself drop. My feet brushed
the wall and twisted. I fell the whole four metres
in a fraction of a second. Crash. Snap. Crunch.
I landed sideways.

The pain was terrible. My left leg and rib cage hurt like crazy. I screamed and screamed, but the sound of the digger drowned out my cries. There was no one to help.

I had always wanted a ride in an ambulance.

I could just imagine it.

People crowded around the stretcher as I was bravely lifted in. Maybe the air-rescue helicopter would land in our backyard.

Or I would get a police escort to the hospital.

Or a gorgeous ambulance officer who looked like the car-wash girl would hold my hand.

But none of this happened. My leg hurt so much that I hardly noticed a thing.

And the ambulance drivers didn't even turn on the siren or go through red lights.

3

Breaking Bones

I **had two cracked ribs and a broken leg.** I spent four days in hospital before they would allow me to go home.

'How did you get to the top of that wall?' said Mum. 'You are just like your father. He is always breaking bones.'

I didn't want to tell a lie so I changed the subject.

'They are digging for the elephant next door,'
I said. 'That's what I was up there looking at.'

'Really?' said Dad.

Mum turned to him. 'I don't want to hear one more word about the elephant,' she said. 'You shouldn't encourage him.'

Dad looked embarrassed. But later I asked him to check out what was happening next door.

'You could fly up and take a peek,' I said.

He shook his head. 'I promised your mother not to say another word about elephants. We had better let it go for a while.'

'Find something useful to do,' Mum said to me. 'Something that will improve your mind. Help you with your school work.'

As usual I did as I was told.

I was laid up in that bed for four weeks with nothing to do but read and think. And the whole time I was tortured by two sounds. One was the noise of that machine on the other side of the wall. Digging, digging, digging.

The other sound was the voice of the car-wash girl singing in the silence of the evening.

Now I hated the singing. It seemed to mock me.

Finally I was allowed up.

I was keen to get out and start digging my hole.

I had to find those bones before the car-wash girl and her family got there first.

But I had a few problems.

Digging was not going to be easy.

The growl from the digger on the other side of the wall seemed to be laughing at me.

Suddenly it stopped.

The only sounds I heard were the occasional shouts of male voices and a dog barking.

'This is crazy,' I said to Dad. 'I have to use crutches, but I don't really need them. I can fly if I want to.'

Dad shook his head. 'Let it be a lesson to you. If you fell from twice the height of that wall you would die. Smash, crash, snap. Dead. You mustn't even fly a centimetre until we have done some serious training to stop it ever happening again.'

'How did you get to know all this?' I said to Dad.

'My father knew about it,' he said. 'He kept it a secret. Like I am keeping a secret with you.'

'How old were you when you first flew?' I asked.

'Much younger than you,' said Dad.

A daggy look came over his face. I could see he was remembering.

'Yes. My parents knew from the start.'

'Wow,' I said to Dad. 'Your parents kept it a secret all their life.'

'Yes,' said Dad. 'My mother knew about it. But yours must never.'

'But what about other people? What if someone else had seen you flying?'

'My parents kept it a secret,' said Dad. 'But it wasn't easy. They went through a lot.'

'It must have been hard for them,' I said. 'Looking after someone like you.'

'I had my uses, though,' said Dad.

'So you had the same problems as me when you were a boy,' I said to Dad.

He nodded. 'The one thing I wanted was for the girls to see me fly,' he said. 'But I couldn't let them see me because I would fall.'

I knew how he felt.

'Speaking of girls,' I said. 'Could you go next door and say hello to the new neighbours? You could check and see if they have found the dead elephant. And find out that girl's name.'

'Sorry, mate,' said Dad. 'But I promised your mother. Any discussion about elephants is out of the question. But I know the girl's name. I met her father at the car wash last week and he told me. Her name is Samantha.'

Ripped Off

And so it went on for another three weeks. Samantha's siren songs on the other side of the wall. And the sound of digging. And in my mind, day after day, I heard the call of the buried elephant.

I couldn't stop thinking about it. Those bones would be worth a fortune.

We were being robbed.

Night after night.

Awake or asleep, I had terrible visions.

Maybe some of the bones were in our place and they were tunnelling under our lawn to get them at this very moment.

Stealing our elephant bones.

I had to know. I had to find out what was going on. I could fly up and peek over the wall again. But if someone saw me it would be my bones that would be buried.

What could I do?

I remembered the school concert.

The tent.

The tent was the answer.

'Ricky boy,' I said to myself. 'You are a genius.
You can check out the action without being seen.
Nothing can go wrong. Nothing at all.'

I could hide inside it and take to the air again.
It had worked once before. Why not again?

That night when Mum and Dad were asleep
I crept out into the backyard with my little tent.
I quickly erected it and crawled inside.

5

Where the Angels Fly

I zipped everything up, but left open the flyscreen netting on the small window. So I could see out.

To be on the safe side I decided to fly the tent over the top of our house. That way it would be less likely that I would be seen if the moon came out. If anything went wrong, I would just fall onto the roof.

But I would have to go higher than our roof
in order to see over the wall. If someone saw the
tent in the sky they would think it was strange.
But I wouldn't fall.

I grabbed the aluminium frame with both hands
and concentrated.

'Up,' I said to myself. 'Up, up.'

A breeze was blowing.

A very strong breeze.

No, not a breeze. A gale.

The wind filled the tent like a stretched balloon.

The frame of the tent was torn from my hands.

I summoned all my mental strength and flew against the side of the flapping canvas. I tried to steer the tent towards the ground, but it was no use. I wasn't strong enough. I felt the tent rocket upwards like an out-of-control elevator.

Up, up, up into the dark sky.

Higher and higher.

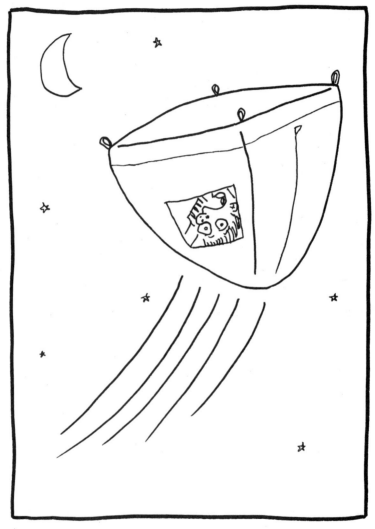

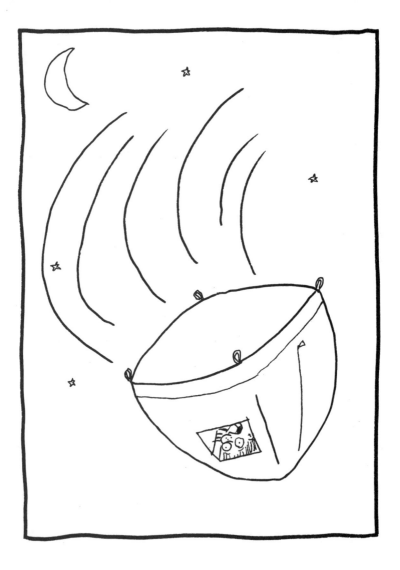

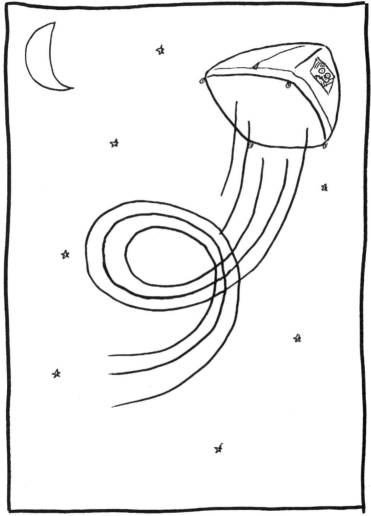

I had to get out.

With fumbling fingers I found the zip on the door and ripped it open. I clawed my way out into the dark night. The tent shot away and vanished into the gloom.

I was terrified. I was flying up there where the aeroplanes go.

The wind shrieked around me. I had never flown this high before. Far below were the shadows of the houses. I could see pinpricks of light from windows where people were still awake.

I closed my eyes and used all my strength.

Down, I went. Down, down, down. I had to
get out of the sky before the moon lit me up.
If someone saw me I would drop to my death.

What an awful way to die. This was definitely in
my Top Ten.

My eyes swept the ground looking for a landmark I could recognise. And there it was: Dad's great wall. And Samantha's house. I could see her backyard and the large black hole where they had been digging.

I fought against the wind. My hair whipped into my eyes. I lowered myself down.

I had to see what was inside that hole. Had they found the elephant?

Now I was about the height of two houses.
I could see…

6

Out Of The Box

Samantha's dog had seen me. I tumbled and spun. I could never survive a fall from that height. The earth rushed up at me.

Crash.

Splat.

Splash.

Was this heaven?

Was this hell?

Was I squashed and flat?

I had landed in the hole in my neighbour's backyard. They hadn't been digging for bones.

It was a swimming pool. They had dug a swimming pool.

Lights came to life in every window of Samantha's house. I heard the back door open. I ran down the driveway and into dark street with the sound of her barking dog at my heels.

I snuck into our house and dried myself in the darkness. Then I crept into bed and fell into a trembling sleep.

In the morning I could see that Dad knew I had been up to mischief. But he kept quiet.

Mum had something to say though.

Something good.

'For you, Ricky,' she said. 'I felt sorry for you. So I started digging in your hole and found this.'

I opened the box.

'It's from an elephant's spine,' she said. 'I looked it up on the internet.'

Mum was very pleased with herself. She was a great mum. I wished I could tell her that I could fly. But Dad would never, ever allow it.

I looked at the elephant bone. I was rapt. I danced around the room. I screamed with joy.

'We found it, we found it, we found it,' I yelled.

So all of my dreams came true. Well, almost. Mum wouldn't even discuss putting the bones up in the front yard. But...

Dad contacted the museum and they came and dug out the rest of the elephant bones. Mum relocated her black-petal poppies before the museum people started digging. They gave us a lot of money to cover the damage.

There was a huge hole in the backyard after they had gone. The three of us stood staring down into it.

'How are we going to fill it in?' said Dad.

I thought of something that would be perfect.

'We don't fill it in,' I said.

I didn't think that they would let me get away with it.

But they did.